For my brothers—Z.E.

For my brothers and uncles—S.S.

Text copyright © 2008 by Zetta Elliott
Illustrations copyright © 2008 by Shadra Strickland

LEE & LOW BOOKS Inc., 95 Madison Avenue, New York, NY 10016
leeandlow.com

Manufactured in China

Book design by Susan & David Neuhaus/NeuStudio
Book production by The Kids at Our House

The text is set in BernhardGothic
The illustrations are rendered in watercolor, gouache, charcoal, and pen

10 9 8 7 6 5 4 3 2 1
First Edition

Library of Congress Cataloging-in-Publication Data
Elliott, Zetta.
   Bird / by Zetta Elliott ; illustrated by Shadra Strickland. — 1st ed.
      p. cm.
   Summary: Bird, an artistic young African American boy, expresses himself through drawing as he struggles to
understand his older brother's drug addiction and death, while a family friend, Uncle Son, provides guidance and
understanding.
   ISBN 978-1-60060-241-2
[1. Novels in verse. 2. Death—Fiction. 3. Drug abuse—Fiction. 4. Drawing—Fiction. 5. Family life—Fiction.
6. African Americans—Fiction.] I. Strickland, Shadra, ill. II. Title.
PZ7.5.E44Bir 2008
[Fic]—dc22   2007049039

Bird

by Zetta Elliott
illustrated by Shadra Strickland

Lee & Low Books Inc. • New York

Today I saw a bird outside my window.
It was perched on the rusty rail of the fire escape
shivering in the winter wind.
I wanted to open my window
and bring the bird inside
where it was warm,
but a sudden gust of wind
blew the bird away.

I drew a picture so I wouldn't forget.

Mama and Papa named me Mehkai,
but Granddad calls me Bird.
That's what he used to call me, anyway.
Granddad passed about a year ago.
Now that he's gone,
his best friend, Sonny, looks out for me.
I call him Uncle Son.
He comes by once a week
and takes me to the park.
Mostly Uncle Son and I
just sit on our usual bench
tossing stale bread to the pigeons.
Uncle Son says he likes talking to me
'cause I keep him on his toes.

I like talking to Uncle Son
'cause he treats me like I'm grown,
not like I'm some little kid
who can't understand anything.
Uncle Son tells me stories
about Granddad,
and all the daring missions
they went on during the war.
Granddad and Uncle Son were pilots.
They used to fly even higher than the birds.
Uncle Son says flying a plane
is the best feeling on Earth.
Except you're not on Earth, really.
You're a part of the sky.

Sometimes on my way home from school
I stop to visit Uncle Son.
He lets me sit at his kitchen table
while I do my homework.
Uncle Son puts on his favorite jazz records
and makes coffee for us
in an old saucepan.
When I'm finished with my homework,
we sit on Uncle Son's lumpy sofa
and sip our sweet, black coffee.

Once I told Uncle Son
I wished I could play the saxophone
like Charlie Parker.
Uncle Son just shrugged.
"That other Bird—he's alright.
But don't you waste your time trying to be like him.
You just remember,
everybody got their somethin'.
And that includes you."

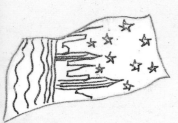

I like to draw.
I'm not real good at it yet,
but I try to practice every day.
Uncle Son says that's how
you get good at a thing—
do it over and over
until you can practically do it
with your eyes closed.

For now I keep my eyes open
'cause I'm still learning
how to get it right.
It's kind of hard.
Sometimes, the picture I draw on the page
doesn't look like the real thing.
Other times, the picture I draw
looks even better than what I'm copying.
That's what I like about drawing—
you can fix stuff that's messed up
just by using your imagination
or rubbing your eraser
over the page.

I draw the things I see in my neighborhood—
buses and trees and buildings and people.
But mostly I like to draw birds.
That's not why they call me Bird, though.
Granddad gave me that name
after I was born.
He said I used to lay in my crib
with my mouth wide-open.
I'd cheep just like a baby bird
in its nest, waiting to be fed.
When I was little, I needed
someone to look out for me.
My big brother, Marcus,
used to do that,
but he can't anymore.

Some days when my folks are working late
I go up on the roof.
I'm not supposed to do that.
But I only stay for a little while,
and I never go near the edge.
I just sit and watch the birds fly.
Most people think birds fly by flapping their wings,
but that's just partly true.
They flap their wings for takeoff and landing,
but once they're up in the sky
they just spread their wings
and soar.

Marcus used to go up on the roof,
but not to watch the birds.
His face would be all tight and angry when he left,
but when he came back downstairs,
Marcus would be chill.
He never let me go up on the roof with him.
But sometimes afterward,
he'd take me to the store
and buy a big bag of chips and two bottles of soda.
Then we'd go to the park and hang out.
I never asked him why his eyes were so red.
I just listened to my big brother
talk about the sky.

Marcus told me there was a place
high above the clouds
where everything was calm and still.
"Sure can't find no peace in the street,"
Marcus would say.
I guess that's why he went up on the roof.

Marcus was real good at art.
He was the one who taught me how to draw.
He'd make fancy words
with all kinds of colors and swirls.
Marcus would show me the picture
when it was done.
A few days later
I'd see it up on a wall near my school.
Granddad called it "garbage graffiti,"
but Marcus called it art.
Granddad said real art belonged in a museum.
Marcus said our 'hood was his museum.
He said the street was where he belonged.

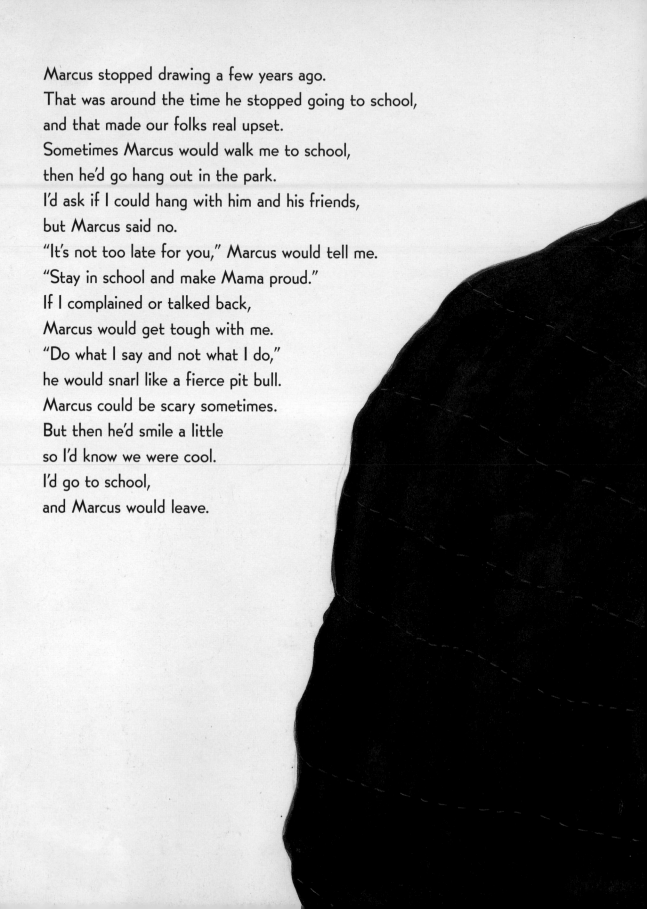

Marcus stopped drawing a few years ago.
That was around the time he stopped going to school,
and that made our folks real upset.
Sometimes Marcus would walk me to school,
then he'd go hang out in the park.
I'd ask if I could hang with him and his friends,
but Marcus said no.
"It's not too late for you," Marcus would tell me.
"Stay in school and make Mama proud."
If I complained or talked back,
Marcus would get tough with me.
"Do what I say and not what I do,"
he would snarl like a fierce pit bull.
Marcus could be scary sometimes.
But then he'd smile a little
so I'd know we were cool.
I'd go to school,
and Marcus would leave.

Whenever I finished one of my drawings,
I'd show it to Marcus.
He would tell me
whether I was getting better or not,
and he'd show me ways to fix my mistakes.

One time I knocked on his bedroom door,
but Marcus didn't say, "Come in."
The door was a little bit open,
so I pushed it
just enough to let my head inside.
Marcus was curled up on his bed,
shaking and sweating.
I asked him what was wrong.
Marcus mumbled something
about needing a "fix."
"Don't tell Mama," he whispered.

I didn't know how to fix Marcus,
so I left my drawing on the floor
and went back to my room.
The only people I ever saw shaking and sweating like that
were the crazy people in the park.
Mama called them addicts.
Granddad called them junkies.
Papa said to stay away from them
'cause people like that would do just about anything
to get more drugs.
I stared at the eraser on the end of my pencil.
Then I drew a picture of me and Marcus up on the roof.
Marcus was better the next day,
but after that night
he started to come home less and less.

One Sunday when we got home from church
all our stuff was gone—our TV, our stereo,
the microwave, my video games,
and all of Mama's jewelry.
I thought we'd been robbed,
but Papa didn't call the police.
Mama sat down at the kitchen table
and put her hand over her face.
Granddad called a locksmith.

Later that night Papa told me
that if Marcus came by,
I wasn't allowed to let him in.
That didn't make sense to me,
'cause Marcus is family and he lives here too.
But Papa said that Marcus was sick,
and until he got better
Marcus couldn't come around anymore.
I asked Papa if what Marcus had was catching.
Papa looked at me for a moment.
Then he shook his head
and held me long and tight.

I try really hard to obey my parents,
but sometimes I break the rules.
A few weeks after we changed the locks,
I heard a knock at the door.
Mama and Papa were still at work,
and Granddad was listening to his radio.
I didn't take the chain off,
but I opened the door and peeked outside.
Marcus was standing there in the hallway.
He didn't look so good.
I figured he was still sick,
but Marcus said he was feeling a lot better.
He told me that he'd be coming home soon.
I wanted to take the chain off the door
and let my brother inside.
But Marcus said he couldn't stay.
He just came by to give me something.
He pulled a bag out of his jacket
and handed it to me.
Inside was a book about birds.
I asked Marcus to wait a minute,
then I ran to my room
and took my best drawing off the wall.
I raced back to the door and slipped it to Marcus.
"This is the best one yet," he said with a smile.
Marcus carefully folded my drawing
and put it inside his jacket.

Then he went away.

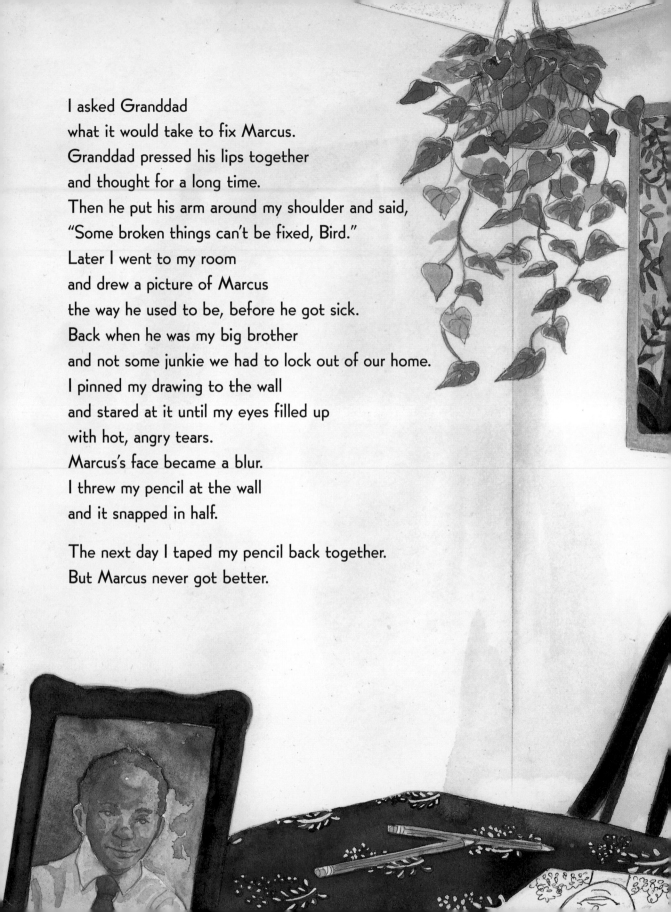

I asked Granddad
what it would take to fix Marcus.
Granddad pressed his lips together
and thought for a long time.
Then he put his arm around my shoulder and said,
"Some broken things can't be fixed, Bird."
Later I went to my room
and drew a picture of Marcus
the way he used to be, before he got sick.
Back when he was my big brother
and not some junkie we had to lock out of our home.
I pinned my drawing to the wall
and stared at it until my eyes filled up
with hot, angry tears.
Marcus's face became a blur.
I threw my pencil at the wall
and it snapped in half.

The next day I taped my pencil back together.
But Marcus never got better.

After the funeral,
Granddad went to bed
and stayed there for a real long time.
Mama said his heart was troubling him,
but Granddad said his bones were just tired.
That was about the time Uncle Son started
to look out for me.

Now we go to the park together every week.
Thanks to the book Marcus gave me,
I can name pretty much any bird I see.
Uncle Son likes the mallard duck best
'cause it's got a shiny green head
like a soldier wearing a helmet.
I like the cardinal
'cause it's bright red with a pointy crest.
When it flies, the cardinal looks like a fiery spark
blowing through the trees.

In the wintertime
it's easy to see the blue jays
playing tag in the branches.
Uncle Son knows a lot about flying.
He told me that birds aren't light
because of their feathers
but because they have hollow bones.
Uncle Son said things that live in the sky are fragile.
We only think that they're strong.
"I wish I could have fixed Marcus," I told Uncle Son.
He just turned his lips upside down
and slowly shook his head.
"You can fix a broken wing with a splint,
and a bird can fly again," he said.
"But you can't fix a broken soul."

Then Uncle Son told me a story
his nana told him
when he was just a boy.
"There was a time," he said,
"when our people could fly.
Back when there were still whips and chains,
folks held on just as long as they could.
But when the body broke
the spirit went free,
and carried the poor soul
home to Africa."
"Is Marcus in heaven
or in Africa?" I asked.
Uncle Son said Marcus was at peace.

Granddad passed two months after Marcus.
Uncle Son said he thought Granddad
went to heaven to keep his eye on Marcus.
That made sense to me.
The next time Uncle Son and I went to the park,
I looked up at the sky
instead of the trees.
The sun was going down.
It looked like a pink and silver blanket
was about to cover the whole world.
"Heaven's that space high above the clouds
where everything is calm and still, right?" I asked.
Uncle Son nodded
and smiled at me.

When I got home,
I drew a picture so I wouldn't forget.